CONFIGURATIONS AT MIDNIGHT

CONFIGURATIONS AT MIDNIGHT

Ralph Gustafson

E C W   P R E S S

CANADIAN CATALOGUING IN PUBLICATION DATA

Gustafson, Ralph, 1909–
    Configurations at midnight

Poems.
ISBN 1-55022-173-6
I. Title.

PS8513.U8C66 1992   C811.54   C92-095251-8
PR9199.3.G8C66 1992

The general editor of ECW PRESS poetry books is Bruce Whiteman.

Published with the assistance of The Canada Council
and the Ontario Arts Council
Set in Monotype Bembo by ECW Type & Art, Oakville, Ontario
Printed and bound by The Porcupine's Quill, Inc., Erin, Ontario

Distributed by General Publishing Co. Limited
30 Lesmill Road, Don Mills, Ontario M3B 2T6

Published by ECW PRESS, 1980 Queen Street East, Second Floor,
Toronto, Ontario M4L 1J2

for Betty

Configurations at Midnight

FOREWORD

The usual method for memoirs is prose. Poetry ensures the least fabrication.

I had no wish to proceed by unrolling the epiphanies of a soul from prelude to revelation. An irreverent sense of irony and comedy dissuades me. But I have, strongly, as all creation has, a rage for order. The Greeks looked at their stars and put them into configurations. So have I mine.

I continue the poetic method of contrasts and counterpoint I used in a book called *Gradations of Grandeur* — the affirmation of life through a sequence of poems expressing the fragmentation and disbeliefs of our times, and the resolution which is joy. The procedure accommodates contemporary experience, the speedily moving mental and emotional succession, the historical and private intrusions inherent in our existence which excite immediacy. With poetry which denies disorder, coherence is not lost.

The level of communication that is current was a problem.

R.G.

North Hatley,
1992

So, to match the moment making
    Death a heraldry
Of which there is no claim,
    The heart and mind brought
Into one so that the sun
    On the day that is,
        Is forever had —
    The foliage of a garden,
        A frond, a flower,
    A happening of importance,
Within the house, a room,
    A glance of glass, a going,
A graduation so compelling
    Dimension is not thought of
    Nor death brought in.

So, I seek the world,
    A renewal of moments:
The far reaches of the world,
    A happening, a stance,
    A music elsewhere heard,
        Each a wisdom:
The ruined temple abandoned of gods;
Three awkward saints on a brick wall
    (*Bassorilievo* sec. x–xi)
    As at Bologna that day,
Jesus and his cohorts, Vitale and Agricola,
Three little men carved by devotion,
    Twice now to seek them out;
The market-street in Paris that summer,
    She who sold potatoes,
        Red strawberries,
    Who smiled in recognition
    Though a winter had passed —
All allegations compounded of memory,
    Life's renewal.

Mohammed's footmark in rock,
Rameses' lights in a Canopic jar,
      The Valley dust;
Under a lid in Lachaise,
      Oscar's wit,
The music's theme *da capo*.

      And hurt ignored:
The little girl, cross-eyed,
Hearing herself a "four-eyed bully,"
Crushing her glasses underfoot —
      The one,
October leaves in the garden,
Who now plants bulbs to have
      Spring's yellow,
      Who knew hurt.

      It is possible:
Spring's announcements,
        Love.

Death?
There is no answer.
Jacob climbs his ladders,
Simon stops fishing,
Martha's fishpot waiting on the stove,
God come down, so made flesh.
Supplicants write it down
On bits of paper tied to the temple's bush —
Balaam's ass stubborn to stick and pull.

Renoir arthritic, tied his paint-brush to his wrist . . .

      On slack pillows,
      Jaw fallen open,
        We smell.

The flesh is sensitive.

It is supposed to be sufficient
To stand in the dark of Chartres cathedral
Under the stained-glass windows,
The sun outside. I have also sat
Nine times in Bayreuth's *festspielhaus*
Four nights together listening
To Wagner's "Ring." Faith is complex.

On the far side of the table Peter and Thomas
And the others took bread from the board and brake it
And swallowed a bit of wine.

So we lean this way and that on the moment
(The moment assumed to be the way we want it).
Church bells ring in Moscow. The Berlin wall
Is down. Desire in grace is epiphany;
Where the meaning is: the August sun
Ripens a field of standing wheat, a horse
Rubs its behind on a beechwood tree.

Being is what the instructed heart has.

Renewal — that reach of ocean, that span of land
Ancestral to the pole, how many times the conviction!
I keep a stone of the Parthenon in a mirror's drawer,
A painted stone of prehistory as if Rembrandt's hand
Were in it; a feather a swan of Avon dropped
(That day in love, she in the yellow-green dress),
Displayed, velvet Arlecchino from Venice next to it
Leaning against the wall in lightweight socks —
No buskin, the comedy not yet over.

   The future:
   The mind as it is

     ✦ ✦ ✦

One future can be dismissed:
That it was all foreseen and therefore wanted.
Not by a long shot: the future
Planned and ordered and called our past?
What was, justified?
Perpetration let off?
Call up the sorrows of the world.

So?

      Free-will. That's the So.
      Job is no answer, wimp
      On an ash-heap in the rain.

It's blustering outdoors. I raise
The collar of my coat and fit in.

      Eaves run wild.
      The brook is wild.
      Accumulation
      On a slant leaf . . .

I go to Washington, Sunday,
To see the cherry-blossoms.
The daffodils are up.

In the National Gallery
Artists have been fixing the world,
El Greco, Goya,
And assorted painters.

The attendance, my nose tells me,
      Seldom wash.
    The image of God.
      (I guess).

(I too prefer creation.)

(But not ideas over people.)

(Soap over steeple.)

✦ ✦ ✦

Just to have her walk into a room
Downs death. The extravagance is so.
What Alexander burned at Persepolis
From a surfeit of wine and love was empire.
I research love.

The racoon rested in the fork of a tree.
I have seen her teach her cubs to open
The trash can, lid locked over,
Hung on the telephone pole against
Recourse. No Alexander needed.
The good smell got to her. The inner
Side of the tomb of Edward the Confessor
In Westminster Abbey once had a hole.
A choirboy put his hand in
And drew out the Confessor's cross.
Many pilgrims sought the miracle.
I feel secure about her walking
Into a room and the lilics clothed.

One might mention the glory of water
Where the stream flows;
The sunfall, then dawn
Over the hills.

Jesus needed water to walk on.

Yeats for his comfort refurbished a Norman tower
To live in as he would, at Ballylee,
Great beams and three-inch planks for improvement.
The house I chose is two levels above
Lake Massawippi with a hedge and lilac tree
Planted forty years ago for words
And silence. Frost had a farm, Voltaire a garden,
Byron nowhere. Love, the place the end is,
We choose early. Keats held his brother dying, Romeo,
The story goes, drank poison, believing love.

Charles Chaplin walked tightropes,
Binoculars backward to the endless circus.

❖ ❖ ❖

I have seen much.
I have never seen
The file of ants
Walking up
A fencepost,
Each carrying
A white petal,
But I hope to.

The taxi-driver I took on Santorin —
The half-exploded island in the Aegean Sea —
Atlantis sunk with all its perfection beneath
The wine-dark sea — the polaroid of him
I took fixed on his windshield fading in the sun,
Not a time he passed but he put both hands
Out the driver's window and yelled "Rejoice!"
"Xairete!"

                The Greeks have a word for it: life!
Permission! whether Hamlet sit and mope
Or Saturn with his fool's crown on, laugh
Bent over and hold his sides.

                        The world
        Is beautiful. Breakers break
        Upon the sands, Orion
        Brilliant across the west.
        We watched the Pleiades of August,
        Showers of stars fell that night
        Over Cavendish Beach . . .

            All her life that lady
            Prayed on her knees, her back
            To the rose-window of the cathedral.
            Biogenetic surgery, I am told,
            Will help, in time.

My father liked fish more than
Answers. He had an answer, a day
In a rowboat, in the sun, fishing,
Pipe lighted, moving the boat
Every once in a while with an oar
Into the shade where the fish are hungry.
I go to Westminster Abbey
And look at Henry the VII's ceiling.
He fished. Ichthus and creation.
Not much to choose between . . .
The context has lost out. London
Is no good, indifference is moved in,
Oxford Street and counterpoint,
Cultures, cigarette ends.

Artur Schnabel gave a piano
Recital at Oxford in 1930
At the Town Hall. The Hall is to the side
Of Great Tom, the five-ton bell
Of Christ Church College that strikes
101 strokes each night
At five-past-nine to toll
The original number of Fellows in.
He was in the middle of Beethoven's
Opus 106, *Die Grosse*
Sonate für das Hammer-klavier.
His wont was to play all four
Of the last sonatas of Beethoven
At one sitting. Impressionable.
He entered the *Adagio sostenuto*
Appassionate e con molto
Sentimento, the third movement
Of the *Hammer-klavier*, when *Great Tom struck.*
He pulled up. Nine. At the bong of twenty,
Left, the *Fuga a Tre Voci*,
Con alcune license, nobility,
Passion, expressivity, all,
All but the untimely tolling lost.

North, where I live, the crocus blooms
For about four weeks, less,
Perhaps, I haven't counted, being
Too busy with coming peonies,
Then eating garden green peas,
Then August Indian corn
(Eight minutes is about all you need
For that, the water already boiling,
That is), far quicker than reading
Remembrance of Things Past. George
Eliot's *Middlemarch* matches
Eating corn though and Chopin's
"Barcarolle," peas . . .

                        profoundest
Sadness to know there is no time.

Keats and his steadfast star, Sterne with his rage,
Dying — Greatness finished, completion lost!

Conditional joy. That's about it.

The grinder turns the gilded wheel at the side
Of the calliope on the corner of the intersection.
We jump out of our skins! The whole of the Netherlands
Leaps out of the sea, the bellows blow heaven up, plug
The polders, hemidemisemiquavers
Sprinkle the air! Out of the silver and ivory
Mouths of the pipes vast processions come.
I drop a gulden in the upturned cap, Rembrandt,
Vermeer, forgotten. Charon grinds away.

       Theme without variation.
       Enter God.

He has a white beard and looks sad.
He wears a nightshirt and is an old man.
He explains everything when you kneel down.
His picture hangs over my crib in a frame.

It's as good as any.

❖ ❖ ❖

No doubt of it, dimension is various.
Of Pound's *Cantos*, scholars will be writing
The poem for him in the thirtieth century
If the treadmill doesn't break down, faculty
Salaries cut, no one to go
To the symposia. Too bad. Pound's
Sea-surge unannotated —
But that's what happens, polymaths
Insisting knowledge be knowledge . . .

"Wild Strawberries"? Yes,
I remember Ingmar Bergman's
Film: the professor emeritus
Who knew nothing. Yes,
I remember: he asked forgiveness.

It's dilation
That's in.
Et alors!
Jean sans terre
Fed his children!
What's society
For, more
Or less? Anon-
ymity exists.
The neglected
Has his name.

(The above rhythm is known in music as *staccato*.
In piano performance Vladimir Horowitz
Is a master of it.
Prokofiev loved the percussive mode. We love it
To distraction.
We will have to learn *legato* and *portamento*,
Grace and continuity
Are out.
Phrasing across bar-lines (not to be disparaged
Or ignored lightly) and love
Uncompensated
Are thought boring, years of practice are needed.
What we do is perfection.)

Caliph al-Mansur of Cordoba never rode
Into battle without forty poets at his side —
A love of enlightenment not equalled in the annals of man —
10th-century southern Spain more glorious
Than idolatrous Europe; baths, mosques,
Thirty-five tons of mosaics blue and gold for one
Mihrab alone to pray in, art unparalleled.
    One hopes the poets behaved abnormally
Without backbiting and with craft and humility.

    I think of Keats and the eternal city, MacDonald's
A few yards away from the Spanish steps.

The beautiful five hundred and fifty-five times?
Domenico Scarlatti did it three centuries
Ago, sonatas spontaneous as the word of God.
Bonnington had no time. Rubens a thousand
Overweight dames, Modigliani,
None. Chatterton lying beneath his window's sill
The vial of poison on the floor. Who knows?
A multitude poets write and not a poem;
Vincent cuts off his ear. Disproportion's
Inscrutable — from here to Carnac's runic stones.

    Henry James died of a simple
    Declarative sentence, Schönberg, Mahler,
    Of an attempt at wit. Pollock, confronting
    A perfect cube. No telling.

        Life is vagrant.
        40% of condoms leak.
        The elephant is doomed.
        Five children a minute
        Are born in Iran.
        I try to get through
        The travellers in front of
        The Bridge of Sighs.

Consider the 2nd edition of the *Oxford Dictionary*,
200 philologists worked for 12 years
Refining the language with timely usages.
Junk food and *born-again* amongst others.

The 27th army moved in
On Tiananmen Square from Changan
Avenue, the Avenue of Eternal Peace,
Wang Wellin calmly stepping
Again and again in the path of the wavering
Line of tanks. No good,
Of course, as much use as the styrofoam
Statue of Democracy erected by the students.
However, comfort can be found.
The Politburo lodged an apology
To Czechoslovakia for moving in
Tanks to crush the Prague Spring
And progress marches on, the Sistine
Chapel ceiling brightened up,
Expert removers planning to remove
The loincloths on the Last Judgment.

Longevity, shortevity,
Domenico is right:
"Show yourself more
Human than critical," he says.
"Your pleasure will increase . . .
Live happily," he adjures us.

✧ ✧ ✧

Collisions and perturbations! Sub-
atomic particles hold their own,
Science assures us, and quantum stability
Demonstrably works. The rose is a rose
Up each spring. Though fish grew feathers,
Each is each — chattering mankind
Got his thumb, dolphins sing.
Blesséd nature that prevaricates —
Profusion piled from pole to pole!
I, lucky Simon, count my stars,
Study tubers where they grow.

Under what Guidance this lily comes
To fruition is not easily
Found out.

I walk churches guardedly, read
Headstones. I am told:
Rest in peace.

There is a paschal bent to the head
Of this lily, a weight to the side
Of unreason,

Repose so happily biased you conclude
Godwork necessary to account
For the transcendence.
I look at this phenomenon.
Absoluteness pulls me
Unwilling in.

That isn't what I proposed. For no
Religious reason and faith,
I go along.

Acceptance. That's it. My mind adjusts
To harmony. I make out beauty
And the weight of dust.

The "supreme fictions"— Wallace Stevens' strictness
For poems — knock one another in my brains,
Earthen pots are earthen pots, cactus
In them cactus, not fleur-de-lis. Poetry
Is as quarks — however it is thought they aren't.
Spurred and trumpeted nasturtiums are pansies never,
They are pine-smelling, falling wanly yellow
Before the upper blossoms have scarcely come
White and inconstant red in window-boxes
Where they stand below cottage green shutters.
In the heavenly sense of course everything is fiction.

There is a duck moving against the stream,
    Excesses of water dripping from its neck.
    Grasses move to the flow of the stream.
        From its hideout below the bank
Surface ripples indicate movement.
    The sun is high, the duck cuts into
    The shade along the north side.
        Noon is gone.

Earlier I had heard the factory whistle upstream
    Where the solitary worker passed
    Carrying his jacket and lunch-pail.
        I was reminded of the lilies
Of the field that toil not neither do they spin,
    The birds clothed and the meek like Solomon
    In all his glory, the earth theirs.
        I am on guard.

The duck is standing on its head in the water.
    Its reach doesn't extend to the bottom
    Unlike the swan's that always seems to,
        Nor do ducks sing.
I watch the duck struggling upstream. Strange,
    The tail is shaking beauty as
    The man with the lunch-pail walks
        Into the distance.

All is quiet in the quiet light,
  Acceptance inheres,
Nothing by itself is apart,
  All is one.

Hills wake to the morning sun.
  Dark withdraws.
The planes of crystal forget their edge,
  All is colour.

Change to the distant west is come,
  Transacts no price.
There is no independence. Ocean
  Commands no arrogance.

The quiet of this room amid the turbulence
And grief beyond this garden's contemplation,
Sun and blue sky, invites the soul's
Wanted conclusion. Just now I cut
Fresh phlox with a pair of rusted scissors,
Lost in gardening and found again,
So that I could have colour indoors.
The humblest flower answers questions.

  My neighbour at the Norseman Inn
  In Ogunquit Beach explains it all.
  "Who started the Big Bang?" he says.
  "The Hubble telescope had a flaw.
  Is your beer cold enough?
  God, that's who." He just
  Might have something . . .

    Back to love.

We were walking around the Marginal Way
  When a rainbow fell to pieces,

Going-green, lessening red —
  Of insignificance to Noah

Now that the Ark was steady and the anchor
    Out, but less to us

Who haul up Simon's elusive catch,
    Ocean's providence.

The impermanence of rainbows, not only along
    The Maine coast, is frequent.

The sun was right, the breakers pounding in,
To hold the glorious moment, getting her
In focus, I backed into the inevitable.

    The blue sky above, a crescent
    Of white cloud a closure round,
    On the balcony, in her day-book
    She quietly writes what has been

        And so, each year,
        The return home.

        Love is possession.
           I watch her,
             By herself,
Raking the grass, the garden's lawn.
        I do not know how to give love,
           Not adequately,
        That knowing love's asking
           She has not less.

        I disinherit love
        That the green grass thus
           Be raked aside.

           ✧   ✧   ✧

Great bursting balls of fire over Venice!
Over Salute, the broad lagoon — Redemption,
Redentore, for all the sins of the world!
Cascades pale green, vertical showers
Red; pinwheels, plumes, falling fountains
Of hope, ascendant crimson inside arcs
Of gold inside spirals, silver, shot
With more silver! The houses out in boats
And barges, O more than any Man though perfect
Could redeem a thousand times, more
Than He, hanging high, reckoned for,
Mamma afloat under Chinese lanterns, trestles
Set with checkered cloth and wine and bread,
Yelling kids and fireworks in heaven!

Chopin's twenty-four Preludes are all we need,
Except that note at the end, that D, that D!

As we sat at the edge of Salute's marble steps,
Lights from the Piazzetta quickened across
The Canal. Grandeur is for a little while.
Our hands together tightened, without fear,
In assertion, the reflection of the lights folding, shattering.

Robert Ford. What assertion
Saved this man, a lifetime dying,
Standing, helped to stand, unable
To stand, atrophy, no fault
His own. How would you explain, Robert?
Dignity, surprise, faith? In despite,
Diplomat for forty years,
Thereza, wife, beside you. The four of us
Drove uptown New York City
To my place to dinner, landing
The wrong end of Washington Bridge,
Destiny in my hands this time!

You and Thereza back to Moscow,
We in Canada; to Samarkand
Eventually, my answering the Russian ambassador
In Ottawa when he asked where
Did we want to go? Tamburlaine's tomb
Of jade and his Schools, who piled up death
A heap of skulls, but you in Moscow
Handling Brezhnev, and the Soviets trying
To keep up with Thereza's ebullience,
Moles or not, going past
The KGB in her bugged car,
Declaring outrage the putting up
A statue to its founder; on imperial
Grounds that the Bolshoi Theatre served
Pink champagne at intermission.
Well, retirement to France . . .
Thereza gone, the New York encounters
Gone. Now, the three of us
At Chateau Poivrière those days
Before you moved from the empty house —
The back of you in that motor-chair,
Betty walking at its side
Down the roadway as I watched,
The fields, the sky, as if permanent!
And talking poetry that courtyard hour,
Of Ottawa, politics in error,
You wondering how you'd lived this far . . .
Never victim to yourself,
Still we write, the Atlantic between,
Poetry and courage the same thing,
Time and assertion always one.

✧ ✧ ✧

The heart understands more fully when the body is still.
Space is exhilaration with motion known.
At rest, time forecloses, meaning is.

> I have watched a mother watch her child walk
> Four steps not moving from her place.

Augustine went aside to pray. The apple
Eaten, Adam begat sermons and sermons,
History down to conclusions. Moses, following
His climb up Sinai, soaked his feet
In distracting water. Demanding quiet from the greenroom
To the stage to play, distracted, Paderewski
Went back, started over again. Stillness,
Without which, God's inattention. The person
On business from Porlock knocking on Coleridge's door,
Destroyed all Xanadu.

> No anthems, please.

> To refresh his soul, Brahms
> Went to lakes and mountains.
> *Oompah* the band played
> At the Thun village lakeside,
> His contented beard overflowing
> So that he did not have to wear
> A necktie. Occasionally
> He raised his hat to the evening
> Ladies he knew in Vienna.

If there are two hundred in the chorus
And one hundred and forty instruments
In the orchestra with eight Wagnerian harps,
> The music is better?

❖   ❖   ❖

The astonishment of being here, of walking a planet,
A harsh birth and a godstroke! I search the history
Of the earlobe, the house of the ant, two
Men in conflict. I sense contemplation.

If one has to make a stand, the end
Is a good beginning. For the start of a day
Try the encompassing fugue at the end
Of a piece of music or if you prefer gardening
Try the trowel on the roots of calendars.

I try on for size the skulls of the monks
Left in the Kiev Monastery
Underground where they lived
Avoiding the soilure of life and fondling
Heaven. The last corpse I attended
The lid was up three hours
For viewing. I need more time.

How to defend oneself against
Loss is not by decision. The walk
By Virgin's farm upland here
In the evening, the pasture gate perched on
Five minutes before going on,
Is wholly lovely as it was.
Remembrance is the heart of loss.
The Bible drives that in — God's
Failure. Job didn't get much
Out of free will, though it worked
Pretty well at Gethsemane.
Imperfection is about,
Willed or not willed, Scott
In his bitter tent come from the Pole.

A brief fall of wet snow,
The sun out again, every
Complex branch hung with glistening
Drops sharp with accurate colour.
I try suspension, number Christmas,
All the eventual story, dismiss,
Implicate contradiction.

At the eastern end of the pillared crypt,
Clothed in scarlet, mitre, gloves,
Lighted by cables and bulbs, Saint Zeno
Lies. The man at the iron grillwork,
Suppliant on his knees, palms
Pressed together, heaves breath.
A box is nearby for omissions. I walk
The nave. Westerly, the rose-window,
The rounding *Wheel of Fortune* red
And blue about the Virgin, stains
The floor of stone. The lower windows
Of shaven amber are forgotten. Sun
Sets the cobwebbed corners on fire.

✧   ✧   ✧

Perfection intrudes, invests.
Youth is a despoiler; age
With its establishments, my father's
Ebony cane had to be
Put back exactly,
Next to the radiator . . .
Symmetry and perfection: the enemy
Of happiness, tomorrow.
From the outside well to her house
Mrs. Sibelius lugged
Pails of water. Sibelius
Couldn't compose hearing
Worked pipes and faucets.
I think of his three daughters.
Milton according to his
Two, talked like a cathedral.
Mrs. Euclid had nightmares.

The razor-blade's in the apple, trick
Or treat, cyanide's in the pill,
The wheelchair's up against the stairway.
Only comedy will do:
The cops are after Keaton; Hardy's
Down the chimney in another mess,
Laurel shut in the closet so dark
He cannot hear. The dazzled drops
Of melted snow are worn-out spring.

My mother used to get red in the face
With laughter, the ridiculous was so great.
What was, I never knew.
Sad by nature, she loved to laugh.
Her china cabinet stood in an angle
Of the dining-room, the glass sides
Were curved. How could glass curve?
She laughed that day as though the china's
Rims of painted flowers had blossomed,
As well they might with her near;
Her goodness had wondrous complications.
Happiness, who remembers it?

What we need are playpens
For children, sharpened pencils on desks
Out of reach of statisticians.
Fire and wheels again. What
Beginnings are. Poems to say so.

Notwithstanding!
Euphoria is in the air,
Come to dine,
Says grace.
The century's done!

The sound was of broken glass. The sentry at the end
Of the Kurfürstendamm looks up. Households
Come out; Leipzig jams its streets; a hundred
And fifty thousand lighted candles burn.
No one packs a gun. Doorways are jubilant.
The file-room's inside out, papers blow.
A bicyclist rides the Berlin wall, a gentleman
Chisels loose a brick. Rumania's flag
Has a hole. Networks prophesy.
The Pope speaks in thirty tongues. The shed
At Checkpoint Charlie's carted somewhere else,
The janitor in it. Cloisters abandon prayer.

In Canada for three days there was wind and snow,
Parliament commended caution; in protest, females
Marched; remarks were made in Senate. The Bay
Lost money, burglars struck. The Coaticook bank
Posted notice: "Fermé. Hold up." Hockey
Prevailed.

Ingenuity does its best,
Undine's godson builds an ark,
One and one, bug and spider,
Leopard, lamb, climb aboard —
Gangplank Eden saved.

Not yet
Beckett's dustbin, humanity dumped?

Investitures whistle down the dark.
Conviction wobbles.

Copernicus put us off-centre,
Astronomer Shapley has tassels on
The milky way, Hubble's bubbles
(Galactic stuffing that isn't there)
Weigh four times a trillion tons.

The expanding universe is running down.
Invisible matter holds it back.
Genesis predicts conclusion.

O "theory of everything!"
"Subnuclear zoo!"

✧   ✧   ✧

I stand by the window. Nothing
Is more at one than this day,
The exactness of winter everywhere,
Footmarks made. Squirrels sit
Appleboughs nibbling wizened
Fruit left hanging by sloppy November.
Twigs shake blizzards. I turn away,
The glare too much to look at. Still
It comes — the black-rimmed stationery.
Now it's McDonagh, maker of books,
Fine-limned books, as if
There was no end. None.

     I think of music, no tonality,
     Tonality lost. Carted. Liszt's
     "Die Trauergondel," that damned carriage
     To San Michele, the double oars'
     Sweep of the waters not interrupted.
     Resolution none, no
     Resolution . . .

It cut like crimson across the west —
The sun, thought of as of no consequence.
I shut my eyes, close off sight.
The slash on the inner dark is there,
The slash, cut across all augury.

❖ ❖ ❖

Methane to oxygen to the first fish, this dappled
Sapphire, earth, goes it alone.

Continuum in perpetuum, immediacy, apprehending:
The grass is green, the grass is green!

At times we love one another, at times. O,
Departure to all the dead well dead!

Who'd skip the cinnamon moon and stars? We scrape
Two sticks together — a blinding light.

Against all brokerage I breathe, scent air,
Oceans, right urgencies.

    The promise of evening was kept, and so,
    Morning, the newness of birds; night
    Did not matter.

    Was it possible signatures,
    Documents, could be accepted?
    Mornings hold

    Stretchings, curtains aside, beginnings?
    Evenings before, supplant starting
    All over again,

    Birds singing all the time
    Repetitively? I too
    Tire easily —

    But accept, accept, a presence of stars
    Nothing to afterwards, even
    Sorrow come to!

We walk through the golden mist, the gate that we knew —
Monet would have painted the light —

The great doorway to the house of Agamemnon,
Of Clytemnestra, the amorous pair

Loved by death. We walk in richness, she,
I, through the Lion Gate, careless

Whether Paris went to bed with Helen
Or not, the morning of more importance

Than Mycenae ruined, Rouen painted — the Argive
Fields heavy with next year's barley

More golden than the dead king's flattened mask.
The sun was out as we had ordered it —

A thousand Troys burning crazily at the other
End of the Mediterranean celebrant,

History on the crumbling Herculean
Walls at Tiryns, nothing to our richness.

She counts the number of buds on the impatiens plant
There on the coffee table. The eaves
Outside have snow.

The set of wooden angels and donkeys with Joseph
And the wise men around Mary
Holding her son Jesus

Bought in Copenhagen, are in place on the mantel.
A risen star is over the verandah.
In fact, hosts of them.

This is the third December she has trimmed the impatiens.
She tests the soil and with the green watering
Can has blossoms in winter.

✧ ✧ ✧

Morning was above the clouds.
No one could have ordered a more beautiful
Floor of heaven, gold,
Unstable gold, to the horizon.
An adorable child kicked
The back of my seat, food
Came locked in plastic, the tray
Was down. The man adjacent,
Talked for himself, smelt.
I managed to uncross my legs.
I had to go. Trolleys
Clogged the aisle. The restrooms
Were full. My heart was full.

That five-day ocean passage spent on the boat
Named after her of the cockeyed royal hats,
Queen Mary, preserve that wasted time! Clocks
Sprung in the rusted glory of getting there!
Deck-chairs, cross-purpose waves, flamboyant
Crepe and wine! wooden horses, the purser's
Gambling "shake the bag," midnight won.
Sam the playwright, wit, and Noel, laughter.

Apart from housebroken children
The human race is not worth it. Barely.

She went into the duplication of diapers
While we were eating; dropped the replaced
Huggies in the waste-basket in my study . . .
By latest count my theories are correct.

I look for a *concierge* who cares,
The *cassiere* who can add.
Once at an outside meal of Nuremberg
Bratwurst behind the cathedral in Munich,
The Bavarian opposite asking for the garnish
Said, "Danke." Unheard of in Canada.
Crudity! Go to London
Now the Commonwealth is there.

Jonathan Swift preferred horses,
Loved Tom, Dick and Harry.

◊   ◊   ◊

Attacked by a crocodile
In the jungles of Mato Grosso,
You my resourceful composer,
Heitor Villa-Lobos,
What did you do? You stuck
A stick upright in the gaping
Jaws and saved yourself
And Brazilian music, that's
What you did, fabulator
Of ten-foot stories. How
The critical cognoscenti
Swallowed your crocodile whole,
Lover of Bach and a large
Cigar (which you light) wearing
My coat with the beaver collar,
Canadian and mestizo out
In the snows of wild Connecticut!
You still take that little
Train of the Caipira in heaven,
Steam out this side,
That, whistle blowing
Saudades, the sadness
At the heart of things ever
In your music, rhythm
Going until the heartbeat,
Valves, wheeze and champ,
Wheel flattened, comes
To a stop? I miss you;
Still conduct your music
Silently as you wished!
Adeus, charlatan
In all that doesn't matter,
Lover of "trips around
The world" and such circuits.

The body of poor old Laurence Sterne
Was dug from the graveyard of St. George's,
Hanover Square, by body snatchers.
An acquaintance recognized his corpse
On the dissecting table. What matter?
Who will forget the making of Tristram
When the goodwife asked at his father's
Most salient moment, *Pray, my dear,*
Have you not forgot to wind up the clock?
And little Shandy's circumcision
When the sash of the window fell down?
And Uncle Toby and the whole of the book
Back-end-to? What possible preservative
Halo can fit the immortal head of him?

Somerset Maugham fidgeted in his bath.
"I will not stutter today. I will not stutter
Today," he repeated, then read Voltaire and Milton
To tune his mind for his morning's limit of prose,
The top hat and ascot necktie worn
To displace his stutter; kept to celebrate
His wife's funeral. An "old Chinese madam
In a brothel," someone summed up the portrait
Sutherland painted of him, wasn't far off —
Hence the apparel, having to have three
Fashionable hits in the West End at once.
The ugly Villa Mauresque he had at Antibes
Is a symbol. We climbed to the top of his house,
The brick room he'd had built so he could write,
The only distracting beauty in the window behind him.
He knew what is what but couldn't have it.
He died rich, first of the second-rate;
Friendly — if it did not interfere, loved
Little, Vuillard and "Born Yesterday."

That great booming voice —
Paul Robeson in concert —
Larry Brown accompanist
Chiming in once
In a while — *Joshua fit*
The battle of Jericho,
Oh, yez, *and the walls*
Came tumbling down
Except that we had to sit
Upstairs on the balcony
In the Ivy Restaurant
Of London that night
Because you were black. We did.
And we went into Surrey — Bramley —
And the four of us played cards,
The cows mooing outside
And the scenery all countryside,
Remote and undirecting
Except to loveliness,
And you slammed down hearts
Like crazy unleashed taking
Tricks and we forgot
That the moon sets, thought it
Still climbed eastward
Where the haystack was and you
Predicted literary
Immortality for me,
And I, that the last two stones
Of Jericho finally
Hit the dust and Ajalon
And Goshen and all the land
Even unto the land
Of Gaza came out in brilliant
Stripes and polka dots
And there were no midnights ever.
How's that, Paul?

And you, sculptor of clay
And stone, Jacob, never
Sir Jacob Epstein thou wert!
You were too natural for that,
Your hands in granite dust
And the reluctant earth, yet
Honour had to invest you.
You saw Lucifer and Adam
Naked (a shilling a look
In a Blackpool basement;
At Père Lachaise graveyard
Your Oscar Wilde memorial
Covered by French authorities
With a tarpaulin — the penis
Broken off for a keepsake).
"Hats on, Gustafson!"
You said that day we went
By taxi to Cavendish Square
Together taking a good look
Up at your Mary and little
Boy over the arch of the Convent —
Never so tender a Mother
And Child cast by anyone,
Verrocchio or after.
And Kathleen (quoting Dante)
At the Isola Bella restaurant
In Frith Street and the one
Behind the Ritz Hotel,
Pointing out models for you!
And your Queen's Gate studio —
The children's heads in plaster
All over the frontroom piano,
Loved and immortal bubbles,
African masks upstairs
Before Picasso thought of them,
Churchill in residence across
The street, you, honest,
Hating all critics.
Mazel tov, Jacob,
Of elemental power
You never thought of!

"Poetic freedom within a basic
Pulse." Shadows murmur in the street,
The evening gone. Exact measure
In spontaneous grace. Hopkins has it,
Ezra, some — if you try enough —
Shelley, all freedom, nowhere to stand,
Browning has it. Jazzmen and horses
Sometimes, sewers of silk.
Not the world theirs but what they do,
Symmetry, fury, out of love.

❖ ❖ ❖

Near Bronzolo north of Verona from Munich,
Clouds dark and pierced lay across
The contour of the mountains, the valley below heavy
With vine rich for harvest, the rows thick,
Hardly breathing left for the gatherers between.
The village spire pointed to God, lover,
We are told, of men, the pastor at hand, portly,
Rich of voice loving the tale good
To hear many times. How they laid
The wire along the pylons, chasms between,
Impossible to tell, but always the way home
Still to be found by the light of the windows on
At night — a fable the pastor, down to earth
Like God on high, did not forget.

                              The sun
Usually burned off the broken cloud
By late morning, marble strata left showing
Too out of the way for easy quarrying.
Riches are the province of heaven, the pastor made known.

I dreamed white whales,
Evil swam the seas.
A black sun was up.
Hate moved: treads
And crushings, mindless loves.
Contempt spat in the food.
Iron crosses burned.
Each thought he was more.
In Oslo, Parleys on Hate
Married hate and love.
I awoke. I got up.
I brushed my teeth, preserving
The confidence of heaven.

In the Bargello we climbed the stairway to the upper floor.
Saint George was there, little David oh my!
And the Baptist shrunk from fasting — David again,
Goliath dripping out his severed neck.
Bronze and marble busy with grace bestowed.
Citizens walked about chewing bread.
Grace outlasts us. Downstairs, Mercury stood
On the wind on one toe; Ugolino,
Starved, and Perseus flaunting his head. I look
For cessation at best — take heaven at its word.

I must look into
This when dead:
Gulls fit ocean,
Ocean, shores;
The hair the head.
Hollyhock-pods
Shattered in October
Have white and red
At the window in August.
Flesh fits sharks.
Men fit God . . .

✦ ✦ ✦

Creation can't be trusted.
Nature should fit the talent —
Schwarzenegger, brainy;
Rachmaninoff, handsome —
Creative talent, nature;
Dürer put a navel on his Adam.

God knows what man disposes!
Picasso's women have two noses.

Adam and Eve in the thirteenth century mosaics overhead
In the southerly porch of St. Mark's cathedral in Venice
Fidget uncomfortably in their first clothes.

Rubens' overweight dames deviously
Fondled as he painted them fill wall after wall
Of the Alte Pinakothek museum in Munich.

Authors should fit their books. Samuel Beckett
Walking in the park on a sunny London day,
His companion remarking the day made one glad
To be alive, answered, "I wouldn't go that far."
His creation, Murphy, dreaming his life away
In a rocking chair, blown to bits when
The gas-plant explodes and shreds him, directed
His ashes be flushed down the toilet of Dublin's
Abbey Theatre. Utterly committed to despair,
Beckett wrote on fervently rescuing his future.

> "Endgame"
> Puts mankind
> In an ashcan.
> The text is revised
> With great care.

I am listening to a Sonata for Flute and Cembalo
By Bach, arranged for piano by Kempff,
Played by Lipatti. Over lucid?

Poor Seyfried, invited by Beethoven
To turn the pages for him at the first
Hearing of the Third Piano Concerto
(Hearing! The ear-trumpets grew larger!),
"Heaven help us!" Seyfried wrote,
"That was easier said than done.
I saw almost complete blank
Pages at most . . . There were what looked like
A few Egyptian hieroglyphics
Which served to remind him of salient ideas."
Heaven serves the indecipherable.

Books? Unto the utmost! shelves
Of them. Multiplied! One
More and we have to move, the weight
More than we can bear, the depth
More than we can plumb, the longest,
Always going to be read, the shortest,
Never enough. Once, putting
My books in order, I failed to notice
An earthquake (minor). Books are fatal.
To turn the pages of his Book of Hours,
Subtly poisoned, Francis the Second
Of France, licked his finger; the pianist
Alkan, reaching from his library ladder
For the Mishnah on the top shelf,
The bookcase fell on him. "No furniture
As charming as books," says Sydney Smith.
I still intend to read Proust.
I keep settling for "Through the Looking Glass."

Of authors there is no end.
At fifteen I had
Three chapters of my novel,
"Westward Ho, with Columbus!",
Done. I got to where
The mutineer dangles
From the yardarm "like a spider
From his web" — a simile
I thought highly of. For proper
Appreciation in Sherbrooke
At the time, there was a visitor
From New York, Miss Catherine Adams,
Author of a book about girlhood.
She was published. My mother,
Experienced, invited her
To tea. She enjoyed it.
She thought my three chapters
"Memorable." Macauley the historian
Has a similar verdict:
"I have read your manuscript
And much like it." Disraeli
Assures an author, he
"Would lose no time reading
His book." I discovered on these comments
Later on though.

"We authors," as Queen Victoria
Said to Lord Beaconsfield.

✧   ✧   ✧

Much is required for an adequate answer:
The cockroach is repulsive and the female
Produces three hundred, four hundred,
Offspring at a time. It hates light.
We may suspect that the life-force
Is not entirely related to Purpose
(Or Original Light as some put it,
Wanting to escape theological God).
How equate the cockroach
With single-minded Benevolence? Dichotomy
Infests the world. Some predict
The cockroach like the Biblical frog
And locust will take over the earth.
The scent of the dog, the reach of the giraffe
And the wings of the hummingbird, of these
There is no need of further praise.
I am halted by Ceausescu of Rumania,
Saddam Hussein of the Arab tribes,
By cockroach and innocence.

I was ashamed killing the spider.
The deed was inadvertent. I was laying
The log on the fireplace when frenzied
By the heat he came out from under the bark
Of the birch and scampered into the flame.
He was gone. Life's surgence is sacred.
Participants of implied perfection,
This one religiously burns opponents,
This one attends the cancerous colon.
I see no subtlety but to accept:
Leave entrails and flame up to Him
And sort the categories out.
I study the cobweb intricate in the sun
And a slight wind and I am perplexed,
Ashamed for no human reason.

In one day the floodwaters rose
Covering the fields each side of the road.
Cattle drowned. Cows were moved
To higher ground, fodder carted.
Snow was heavy all winter
And now melted. Each stone
Swept spirals of colour, embrasures
Spilled back to green stabbings.
A leg stuck up. Crows came.
Accomplishments of spring were cancelled.

Life subject to death. I walk along
This cornice of field, easeless, aware of what
We have achieved: a jewelled egg, a laced shoe,
Versailles — leave to the new century
Immovable perfections, smokestacks, AIDS,
Equations to set belief at rest.

    The uses of detraction are a Bible
    Diminished, the worm knotted in the sun
    That thrives, duplicates, buried,
    Limbless, eats dust. Jonah
    Threaded one on the hook of the line
    Of his fish pole, pulled out Eden.

The beauty of the world is not over.
Unexpected, overnight
Snow came. An hour and the world
Was covered, along the branches, thick,
Along the fence, the corners, under
The moon the path to the roadway, white —
The mole did not venture out,
No mark until the sun should come —
White, to the farthest recesses, man
Himself could not refuse the abrogation,
The gift! Absolution is thought of,
The possible truth of the breath of his words,
Of the fall of an interval of music bringing
Succession. This night of snow, one night
And the heart is itself in exactness.

The poet Louis Dudek and I
Had turned down the Niger River ravine
Near his house in Way's Mills.
We had a discussion to settle: why
God? and if He wasn't would
We have to have Him? We decided we had to,
We couldn't discuss God if He wasn't
And walk down the gulch of the Niger
In broken dappled sun and approach
An adequate conclusion. I lost a glove
During the discussion. The left glove.
What to do with what was left
Was what the walk in the dappled sun
Came down to: to find a perfectly
Lost left-hand glove to go with
The right in the time that we had.

O I give farewell to philosophers and reason,
It is the mind that fumbles, alternates that give way.

The cobweb, the crystal of snow, the chameleon's eye,
These are consistent. The whorl of a shell,

The eyelash, these are simplicity.
I dispense with adumbrations of dust.

Sands are; mountains are. Whoever
Wants metaphor has likelihood.

The scheme of the potter is true configuration,
The openness of the flower and the warmth of sun

Are relations, morning, evening, beyond persuasion.
The very setting out was done in sorrow.

The promulgations of the heart are revised in accordance.
In the sharpness of night are Orion and his bow.

❖   ❖   ❖

The ambiguity of compensation came
From the surgeon who put my pacemaker in.
"I feel fine," I told him with what I thought
Was wit, "except for deterioration." He put
The stethoscope down. "You have your imagination."

Ned Adams my friend who had girth
And was oblivious of it, who brought his films
To my father's studio to be developed,
Day or night, the sunniest, wore rubbers
And carried a folded emergency umbrella.

Earlier, the plane ride had nearly
Done me in, a 1926
Open Cockpit Plane it was called,
Privately owned by Bud McRae.
The local runway was at St. Hubert
Outside Montreal (saints
Are everywhere in Quebec).
It was twenty-one years since
The Wright brothers. I sat in the rear
Cockpit. Bud stood on his seat, waved
His arms in the air, both of them. The plane
Tilted. My cap caught in the struts.
I laughed carelessly, the big guy,
Virtuoso.

The ride (commercial)
Five years later from Oxford to Hanover
Was in an enclosed plane. I opened
The window (an advancement) my side.
The stream spoiled my right antrum.

The same error was made
At the Plymouth Brethren funeral
Of my playmate Ruth Davis.
It was with "great pleasure"
The minister opened the eulogy.

I once queued up in mid-August
Cold at the ruins where Caracalla
Took his baths. Tebaldi
As Tosca could scarcely protest
Death. Clogged nose.

I kept promising myself to go to Nepal.
Other people did. I wanted to see
Everest, Nupse, despite the height.
For years I had gone up mountains
In my armchair, dared the cablecars
Of Switzerland, had stationed the Matterhorn
In my window at Zermatt. There it was,
Whymper's fatal first ascent,
Hudson's shoe dug up from the ice
In the town museum. Old Croz
Dead and hapless Hadow. I have gotten
To like the familiar — no wish to see
Calcutta, who would? or the Taj Mahal.
I have seen the Parthenon,
Ponce de León's Florida,
The roseate spoonbill. Like Humpty,
I keep on sitting content
On the slate coping in my garden.

✧ ✧ ✧

Diminution's the thing, it chastens
Ambition and suchwise aspirations.
Arranged by Liszt for piano solo,
Dohnányi played for me one day
The "Pilgrim's Chorus" from *Tannhäuser*
With a grapefruit in his right hand —
Teeyum teeyum teeyum in the treble
Down; the black-key *Etude* by Chopin
With a hairbrush, *tum-tum-*
TUM, etc. Who could wish
For more? He was a musician after
My own heart, he honoured solemnity
With perspectives, as Arthur Loesser
Did, giving recitals of the world's
Worst piano music. Caruso
In the midst of *Traviata*
Passed a raw egg to his soprano.
Poor Violetta, it did her
The world of good.

We swam at Smyrna — where the Greek girl
Lived whose son was Homer — in Izmir's
Glass-walled pool. The sloping Turkish
Alleys led to Homer's town.
We watched the sun set in gold
Over the Aegean sea, listened,
The lap of Triton's turmoil touching
The edge of Miletus' marble steps.

The longboat's keel strikes the shallows!

Pergamum is grass; Didyma's
Amphitheatre broken, Apollo's
Shadows no longer Persia's pride.

Einstein loved his violin
As any equation. Playing
Sonatas with Godowsky the piano
Virtuoso of his age,
Einstein lost a measure,
Godowsky his cool. "What's
The matter with you?" cries Popsy,
Slapping the lid of the piano,
"Can't you count? One
Two three four.
One two! three four!"
Such is the pulse of the universe.

I watched him as the Honorary Oxford
Degree in latin went over his head.
His eyes twinkled relatively.

I once said to Charles Chaplin,
"You are one of my heroes."
Oh.

    Mr. D'Attili
    Of Dumont, New Jersey,
    Is happy. He sits
    In his basement appraising
    Violins, violas,
    Cellos. He's happy
    Just holding them.
    As many as possible.
    He does not want to be
    A millionaire.
    Maria his wife
    Sifts the requests
    From four continents
    Made to consult him.

Hucksters, critics, whoever forever
Breaks what he picks up are a part
         (I suppose)
Of this engaging beautiful world and (perhaps)
Are eminently worthy of affection
         (I hug you, O huckster)
Especially if they have only one
Last heirloom dropped rinsed
             From the pan
             (O Chinese Pan!).
I am not talking of awkwardness
             But of those who don't care
In a world uncaring enough as it is
             (Hear here, bassoons and tubas):
Of slobber got rid of nearest at hand,
             Deconstruction
             (O academics),
Beer-bellies and abandoned hypodermics
             (The beach was miles),
She who keeps saying "You know"
             (Not till you tell me, dearie),
The stoned, not the thrown-at,
The gesture and not the commitment,
Batter, not the silence
             (Blessed be *pianos*),
The spitter, not the spitten
             (O baseball!).
May all be considerate,
May all have humility.

O the unbalance of things,
Marsalis and his super trumpet.
"He didn't kill nobody, you know . . .
I was like nineteen or something, man —
You know, wild. I didn't care."
He speaks lovely, eh, man?
Blow, Gabriel, blow!

                    ✧ ✧ ✧

And so it is, there is, no,
There is never enough of equity,
Of walking the measurable earth,
Stones against the impressionable heel,
The pathway, the inlet, water and soil,
Both, next the shore; deep
Snow, reluctant. Moments remain.
Grief, yes. But not what
I can remember, those moments — the Acropolis.
The two of us taken by the wandering photographer
Seated on the fallen marble of Athens,
Arrived at happiness. Lake Vänern
In Sweden, the moon full gold,
The Göta Kanal's three nights . . .
Ivalojoki, the river that side
The Arctic line of Finland's sun,
The sauna's hot stones and madness,
Ice, the river jumped into . . . Vesuvius'
Stygian crust walked on. And

The haymow that was there;
Easter, the dough for bread risen
Over the warm register, these
Remembered; particulars.

Each season's gift returns, the furrowed
Row, the travel's shape, the need,
Egypt's

Seasons wherein the gods reside,
The noria turning, the altar at Abu
Simbel

Burdened with sheaves and fruit, taking
The striking sun. The lilac, covert,
Double

Waited-for. Only man
Out of season surpasses this.
Listen,

You will hear the bone snap.

The body was five thousand years old,
Uncorrupted as if asleep yesterday.
He was untouched, no cerement, priestly resin
Or three-lid coffin — he lay there as himself,
About twenty-five.

                        The burial room was down
The twenty-rung wood ladder near
The Chephren pyramid — Sharik Farid (his son
Was turning Eliot's "The Waste Land" into Arabic)
Took us down — the excavated chamber
Kept hidden, I suppose, because the parched
Depth preserved the perfect nakedness.

    Behind the partition of glass his eyes were closed
Quietly, the arms folded, his toes perfect,
The sex rested in the groove of his thighs as if
After having love. The penis, Farid told us,
Corrupts first.

        I wanted to call his name.

    This was before we had climbed up
    Inside Cheop's empty pyramid, saw
    Hathor with the cow ears
    In her temple up the Nile and passed
    Akhenaten's city crumbled to dust.

        What shall we say?
        I have no pyramid?
        Said words
        Silence hears?

                    ✧   ✧   ✧

Ecstasy is as the meaning
Of that morning,

Not abstract Plato — someone
Sawing wood,

Sawing crosscut birchwood
His mind on dust

Drawn up into the air,
The sorting sun.

In the shallows fish
Swam
Indirections.

The current passed
Stones
Capped silver,

Pulled attached
Shadows
Immeasurable.

Nor was silence
A metaphor
For summer
Passed,

Thumbed autumn's
Shortness.
The silence
Was love,

Extensions of nothing
That is nothing
Without
That love.

❖ ❖ ❖

Let me bring you up to
Aunt Ida Carpenter married
To Uncle Henry Marsh
Who was deaf as a post
And ran the general store
In Norton Mills about
An hour from Lime Ridge
Where I was born. Norton
Mills is in Vermont
Where my grandmother had my mother,
Gertrude Ella Barker,
In the bedroom partly in Stanhope,
Quebec, the two villages
For all purposes one —
My mother therefore born
In two nations, Canada
From sea to sea, the U.S.
Top to bottom.

My father came from Växjö,
Sweden. He got a job
In Lime Ridge in the grocery
Store of the Lime Company
Whose superintendent was
My grandfather, James Barker,
Whose daughter he married for love.
He loved quality, wore
Kid gloves to pile
Cordwood and had no use
For his brother August who,
On his way to Vancouver,
Stole his ivory flute
And brass bed. August
Died young. My father
Lived well into his nineties.
Quality, pursued, pays.

With reference to my father
Taking twice the arsenic
He should have, to speed the cure
In his legs — and to his brother John,
Dynamiter at the lime kilns,
Stuffing the cliff with twice
The dynamite stipulated
To cut his workload
In half while he had lunch,
A cow and the railcar trestle
Down to the pit demolished —
The rumour is Swedes
From Smöland Province are stingy.
I had this from a fellow traveller
On the ferry going from Stockholm
To Finland. He said, as well as
Being stingy, Swedes
From Smöland Province where
My father and his brother were born
Are mean. He didn't know
My father and John doubled
Life to save time.

Alas, for ignorance.

> My sister who was four years older
> Didn't much like me tagging
> After her when she played. She had
> A den behind the lattice trim
> Of the back verandah where she pinned up cutouts
> Of Hollywood movie stars; she wore
> Stick-out false hair-buns
> Each side of her head where the ears are.
> Girls talked. I was Tarzan
> Clinging just barely to the boulder the glacier
> Had left across the street. I was
> Also John Carter, Warlord of Mars,
> Madly in love with Dejah Thoris.
> My lieutenant was Tars Tarkis
> Who was green and had four legs.
> The exploits are among world literature.

The house screen door slammed behind him
To keep the summer insects out, my father
Stood a moment to get out his pipe, then scratched
The jamb not thinking of the fragile paint bubbles,
The match flaring crimson an instant, the tobacco
Catching, he standing still to protect the puff,
Then going — walking in the evenings down the hill
To the studio. Where it ran into Montcalm Street
The street was named Wolfe until the French stopped
That. Except for the sidewalk it wasn't then paved.
In August the sweet corn in the garden back
Of the house was higher than I was — in the middle of a city.
He turned off down Frontenac Street,
His legs not too good, but you did not know it,
Swedish obstinacy, independent of emotion —
He liked emotion well enough when it was not
Made an instruction. He loved a straight-stemmed
Pipe . . . It smelled good. I still have it.

Remembrances that offer us back: the broken porcelain
Figure mended in the corner china cabinet;
REGULATOR plastered in gold letters
Across the glass front of the wall-clock's
Pendulum which I scratched away with a pin . . .
Appearances: the lace she wore; the song-sheet
Yellowed in the attic, the box one day
Dragged out: the marriage announcement, the shallow silver
Bowl only of a spoon; between tissues,
The dress folded, the gloves, forgotten . . . lavender . . .
The leather volume of *Best Loved Verse*
The spine broken. Old letters. Hear me.
I am better than all of this, better . . .

✧   ✧   ✧

Let us translate music:

Anger then ecstasy, meditation,
these proofs there are until the spirit
unregulated establish what
has already been known:

Dominion of God and Light
that in fragments
is our use.

Abstract thoughts! these in sensation,
music brought down
in substance manifest.

(Scriabin *Sonata 5*)

Equivalents of tiny bells.
Inquiries of truth and time?
But pacings, beside the pool,
          Delicate incense
Spilled inadvertently but
The tiny bells among the
Gongs, equivalents! equivalents!
The gods will hear
                    will hear . . .

(Debussy "Pagodes")

Dolce:

Walking slowly, compensation beside
a pond? yes, a border walk —
the rippled surface
quickened, crowded coming,
touched!
          Enough! State it!
          Gratings!

Dolce come prima:

the water touched.

      Overreach, overreach!

Regular pace, ordered insouciance,
kids dancing to tunes, kids down slides
and skipping better keep beat
or whistle through your fingers,
kicking small heels carefree
the balustrade over the Moscow River
comical, slidings and love (a little),
        but keep time!
the future is here, the future comes!
               (Prokofiev *Sonata 8*)

❖ ❖ ❖

"An absence of being," the Greek says of evil.
More! more than a want of sun,
As a shadow is more, is that which is hidden;
My shadow grows longer, dark insistence
Lengthens me, the equivalence of a century
Is as nothing, my breath enough for only
Dreams of no substance, music unheard.

The gods of Jidda and Jerusalem
Are more than an absence of history
As goodness is more than that wafer
Eaten. I shall go out in protest,
Hang petals up with the full moon
Up, crush through snow, exhibit
Being, words salt on my tongue.

I went out to see if the buds had roughened
The lilac bush. The sun, the April
Air, was mild. March was gone,
The year's harsh winter. Yellow
Along the forsythia branches was tense,
Smoke was reported in the woods where
The maple's sap is boiled. The first
Of the crocus was up. There was evidence of later
Primrose. Immortality was ready,
Double white from the lilac bush.
Whether I was too early thus
Going out or the maple tree's
Scarlet was fallen, wouldn't matter.

    What a conclusion, kettle of fish!
    Digging in toes against the tide,
    Curtains up in the rinsing morning,
    Down again and when, at night!

        The gull is concision.
        Fluttered, windshaft
        Lifted, gets updraft.

Scans sandbeach,
Fence, the green
Garbage can,

Comes quark-cry down,
Eyes apprised,
Sidewised . . .

Yanks refuse out —
What it loves.
Loving, reaves.

Walking landscapes won't work.
I have tried it, walking up
Virgin's Hill past the farm,
Resting ten minutes seated
On the barred gate overlooking
The lake; going on. Whatever
Brief that evil promulgates
Fence-sitting helps. Breathing
Air is assurance. Calamity let loose
So faith can be armtwisted, whirlwinds,
Nothing can improve. Correctible
Hurt is man's, not undone
By *tu quoque*, piety, or burning
Joan. I got off the top rail
Sorrow deeper for the lovely view.
Defiance, charitably plugging holes
Lefy by omissions, only will do.

Who heard Beethoven's Ninth
In Berlin that Christmas, heard assurance.
Promoters sold pieces of the wall
Defiant one side as mementos.

Philosophy fails, Absolutes.
Only order, "a rage for order,"
Will do, undoctrined anger,
Adam in his petulant garden,
The mud good and the working sun
Good and the legislative body,
And knowing the house could be straightened with a hammer
If he had one, eating apples worth it —
Fish and fowl and cows and orderings,
Bee-lines, Adam could not name them
Fast enough: loins and love.

He settled down: the spider's selection
Of seclusion, the watercourse salmon
Die in, the hive's retrieval,
Questions of actuality: Schubert's
Inspiration, Cézanne's stroke,
The elephant's domesticity?
All is poetry, poetry.

❖   ❖   ❖

Without warning as I looked up
A burst of broken light centred
And splayed in a thousand shatterings of coloured
Vision, impressions on impressions,
As music — the whole an incandescence,
Implication. I was without questions,
Assertions, the instance a farther room
Of hers, the chair, the orange leather,
Only the reading lamp of the antique
Desk on. Against logic,
The flaring glass of the empty Orrefors
Vase cut in all directions
Refracted as fire. It was surety.
Without compliance. Of no use.
It was light, silence of light,
It was flame.

Re-Harakhty, God
Of fire and of the sun.
This:
More light.

✧   ✧   ✧

O what women bitter at heart
Stand at the edge of the barren fields?
Old women in bitter shawls,
Babushkas tied under the chin.
It is cold. Life spent bending —
Water from the yard, in pails, sickness
At the bedside. The horizon here
Is forever. Bearing. Bearing can be
A bitterness. Only at the fence
The interval, talking . . . The hair falls
Loosely; it was black, raven,
If you will . . . The man of the back country
One January passing along the road,
The road going to Yasnaya Polyana . . .

❖   ❖   ❖

And human beings
Living in imposed
Filth in Rumania.

Repetition! Inexhaustibility!
Monet and his serial grainstacks,
Rouen's cathedral front in unsuspected
Light, each spring, each flake of blustering winter,
The very hunks
Discriminations of experience!
And adamants of life, craftiest subjections;
Mould and accurate templet, contradiction!

Christian battles
Islam, Islam
Battles Jew.
Muslim bloodies
Rama, Ulster
Fights the Pope.

Abolish god.

It's original sin alright, perfection
Out, dishevelment in.

Consider copulation, joy
Unending, the bottom-line of love,
The silly friction accession to heaven!
Guilt assigned to innocence,
Naked babies washed at the door!
The rounding world is in jeopardy. Sober
Ecstasy, that's what's called for, this intricate
Flesh worn in the cause of heaven.

It strikes at any moment, life,
In the midst of choosing; standing humming
Silently, minding the sun's business,
Dividing intimacies; fifty-five miles
An hour, no miles per hour.

Of all the vanities there is none
As breath. North and the frozen darkness,
The southern rose halfway open
Beyond compare — this total —
Incalculable time, Tuesday next —
None is as breath. "As sparks fly upward,"
Says the Book. "A little folding
Of the hands to sleep." Proverbs, Job,
No denial. That day finally
As wished: time to get there
Not long enough, not long enough there.

Videlicet: what is less glory
Than a thread-leggéd spider scurrying
From the inner bark of a flaming log?
A man dying not knowing when,
That's what. The log was carried
From the dark cellar where it lived;
He, with god-imaged promise,
Carried in his mother's womb
Pommelling for lack of air,
Helpless obeisance to finality.
The end should be set out,
Now, for lovers, both at once,
Without penalty for being.
Should it not, should it not?

It's no use. We can't compete, not
With a short-lived gooseberry, not with C-natural.
A maelstrom of petals, a flash of water,
Nature's beyond us — what quality we have
Is imposition, cogitation.
The advantage is nature's. We are vanity, neither
Jubilant dolphin, impervious duck. We have
What the preacher says, that I have mentioned.

Sleep done, sunstruck
We wake to morning,
Rattle in the kitchen,
Milk bottles;

Enamoured of fresh beginnings,
Stalling, yawn,
Stretch out of yesterday,
Have mortality:

Blue oceans, the ways
Of going done,
Exploit old
Gravestones.

✧ ✧ ✧

An ordering of accurate words
    Will do.

To Scriabin, F$^\#$
At 383 vibrations a second
Was bright blue, to Rimbaud, each
Vowel, a different colour — sensation
Held to true account, thisness
Exacted, meaning in exactness transcendent,
Each to each, as time, as breathing
Is, as tide suggests the moon,
Stone, Druids' haulings, Stephen
Martyred, though stone is stone, indurate,
Impassive, beyond harmonics and itself.
Double allocation, as words
In poetry, depth and degree of breath
Their meaning, let metrics clash as they will,
The rhythm right and the meaning music,
Rough or smooth, whatever is heard.
Scan as you will; how it is said:
Delight — not self-conscious, sloven,
Not constrained, the heart the temperate
Power; emotion has its own
Degree, alert for the vowel, the consonant
Unobtrusive constancy.
Movement, resonance, heard silence!
English, grand unparalleled music!

Image against image, spilled
Quicksilver! that's one way,
Velasquez, Pound, Klee;
Narrative breathless, another, a going
Richness: Chopin, Goya, Liszt;
The third as music (almost solely —
Syntax to the devil if need be):
Stevens, Kandinsky — all those
Who hate tin ears. *Ut doceat,*
Moveat, delectet, Shakespeare
Incomparable! So it exists this poetry.

❖ ❖ ❖

It was miles in to the Selkirk Range:
Mountains lifted from oceans. Snows
On the upper levels melted made
A desolation, held marshland.
We got to it, faith worked, without
Thinking of it; we were together;
Instinct for affirmation turning us
West where Amethyst Lake was
And beauty was. The sun was out.
Inside the edge of the morass, surrounded,
It was no good. We caught our breath.
I rested on the log half in the mire.
She handed me the small flower.
I had likened the dusted black of the stamen
Within the waxy petals to spend.
The garden name of the flower there
Is Single Delight. By midnight
We got back to Mount Edith Cavell,
To the chalet we had started from.
We slept late. Next day,
Boots dry, we turned over the map,
Going on, questioning.

❖   ❖   ❖

The time might be after that early frost
Of May which harms many of the blossoms.
No, we are not sure anywhere,
The countdown is without opulence,
The aggressions of summer do not help.
We are left only with theory. Note
That the radiate apple petals did not
Need even a fragile wind to fall.

Safe at home, her beside me! Hours
Still to go until she is back, music
On the stereo, in the middle of the Mozart
The bellow of the cow not ours a half mile off
Full of milk and Uranus beaming facing
The rocketed telescope amid the unblinking stars.

Committees re-position commas. I wish
She was home, the doors unlocked all over the house.
It's winter. My heart aches — the logs burning,
Snow falling, happiness possible,
Salt oceans tumbling and so on . . .

It is the gayety she has, going off,
Her umbrella aslant, loving the thunder,
An unduckable challenge to calamities
Should they exist. She knows, of course
She knows, how sorrow when least wanted
Enters in, how shoes, eventually,
Get soaked, as a child she knew: worse
Than indifference, love that demeans.
Everyone knows sorrows. A birthright.
She angles her umbrella sheltering
The world, wears her best shoes
In the rain — the ones in two colours,
Grey and green brought all
The way from Venice, the shop at the next
Corner just up from the Rialto bridge
Where Antonio did not know why
He was so sad. She does.
She has gambled sorrows cornered.

O I shall prove that the crisis
In the Middle East is false.
I have turned on the footpath lantern
That works with the lamp on the verandah.
The three steps up
To the walk are well lighted.
It was to the postoffice she went.

To mail a birthday card.
The power of love is more
Than theory. She is back on the verandah.
We watch the blue-footed
Booby on TV
Dance. The bird reminds me
Of Joplin's piano-jig.

Have you seen the blue-footed booby dance —
One foot, the other, Joplin's ragtime rocked?
You must see that before you leave for heaven.
And the penguin in white-tie slide on his bottom
Slippery ice down to the sea for fish?
That too is worth interrupting
Adding and subtracting for. The prospect alone
Cancels any impulse to get it over with. Watching
The hummingbird confront a tipped scarlet
Trumpet will do this, a skyscraper
Going up, oil-patches watched.

Notice that the scales of drying fish
Wet in the sun, are iridescent;

That lack of stones deepens water.
The grain of wood sustains study.

It was as if I tasted cinnamon examining
The nature of mahogany.

Snow is a fit subject for logic.
The look of an equation is sufficient.
One could do worse than propound
The shaded moss-side of a boulder.

Within a building a light shines,
They work at night. No one talks.

❖ ❖ ❖

Hamlet's shadows, Akhmatova's ghosts,
Old sorrows, what are old sorrows to me?
The arras is drawn, St. Petersburg survives.
What phantoms matter? Cassandra's loves,
Richard's princes in the Tower, the staircase
Silent? Niobes weeping headstones,
Eurydice, Orpheus' broken lute? All
The ceaseless sorrows. Endurance only matters,
Mephistopheles' shrug and the plunge where
The last ruby sinks in the pond mossy
With forgetfulness. Let us sit and
Contemplate while horses' hoofs pound
Riderless across apocalyptic skies.
O vasty emptiness, sorrows of Lebanon,
Candelabra gutter above cloth of shrouds!

❖   ❖   ❖

FUGUE:

Counterpart to all we had seen:
Sole and a lemon at the Mitre
In Oxford, going from country to country: a fifth,
Sixth masterpiece

Come on, remembered men's work
Or anonymous. I learned what I
Had guessed: love matters, food is necessary —
Hard-shelled lobster

And a potato, or metaphor. I eat the means and seek
Ends, simple enough
To what only is: Greek Ictinus building
Proportion; Venus

Standing on her birthday cockleshell,
VINCENT in big letters,
Anonymous "Sumer is icumen in" —
Whatever's given —

Schumann who couldn't compose, Clara who couldn't
Compose, each within earshot,
Who loved each other; Monet and his painted
Boat secure

Among lilies where the reflected willows weep.
The richness of the world, O world!
The Lord's prayer engraved on the head of a pin
As if heaven could come!

The achievement found at the end of things:
The lessening of an ability to know.
Mist on a clear night of the moon,
Truth of a change troubling the exactness
That is itself. World and fatal
Heaven, the paradox . . .
I am next to midnight,
Almost I hear the bell toll —
Assurance I could do without.
I have no answer, faith the warrant
Of intransigence I would not leave.
Sensation claims me, I leave my love.